kiss him, he's irish

emma bray

one

. . .

Thomas

I'M SITTING in a coffee shop sipping my dark brew. It's black just the way I like it, but I feel like a pansy sitting here at a delicate little table across from my buddy Derrick. I'm more of a get it and go type of guy, but my best friend and business partner is all hung up on a little barista who works here, so I agreed to sit with him at his request so it's not so obvious he's stalking the hell out of her.

I try not to growl as he fumbles to fit all the papers he needs to show me on the tiny table. This place is counterproductive to business. I'd much rather be back in my office where we've got plenty of room.

"Derrick," the severity of my voice snaps his head up. "This isn't really the appropriate place for this type of meeting, man."

Derrick scowls at me before glancing back up at the barista he's obsessed with. My eyes flick over to her casually. I admit she's a cute little thing with mocha-colored hair and caramel-colored eyes. I just don't see what all the fuss is about and why Derrick is willing to damn near jeopardize our careers over her.

"If you just give me a minute to get all this sorted…" Derrick mumbles to himself, still shuffling through papers like a moron.

"Seriously, man, we'll pick this up in my office. I'm not dealing with this here." My tone brooks no argument, and I watch as Derrick's huge shoulders slump with defeat. He knows I'm right. What's more is I'm technically the boss. While we're partners, I own a bigger share of the company, so my vote has more weight than his.

With a sigh, he scoops all the papers up in his hands and works to stack them together before thrusting them back into the manilla folder. All the while, he keeps a close yet surreptitious watch on the barista.

I roll my eyes at him. "For God's sake, how long are you going to keep stalking her? Why don't you just go over there and ask her out?" I don't get Derrick's infatuation with this girl, nor do I get his hesitation to let her know what he wants. Derrick's never been this high-strung over a female. He's usually laid back and easy with the ladies. And with our success and good looks, neither of us has any problems getting female companionship if we desire it.

My buddy glares at me, and I let out a good-humored laugh, enjoying his discomfort.

"What, lad? This chick totally has you by the balls, and you haven't even spoken to her."

"Shut the fuck up," he growls at me, his brogue becoming more pronounced with his irritation. Hell, I can't say anything, though. Mine does too when I get going about something. Piss us off and that Irish comes storming out.

I hold my hands up in a gesture of surrender, though I can't keep the shit-eating grin off my face.

Derrick and I have been through a lot together. He's been my friend ever since we met back in grade school in our homeland of Ireland. Once we both finished high school, we attended university together and then scrimped and saved every penny until we had enough money to start our own business, which is now proudly headquartered in the great old US of A.

We've always been there for each other. He's a true

friend, and he knows I'm just busting his balls. I'm honestly happy Derrick has found someone he cares about, but I still think he needs to make a move on the girl before another man does and he goes into a murderous rage.

My eyes roam back over to the object of my best friend's obsession. "Seriously, though, man. She looks nice enough, approachable. Why don't you just—"

My words fall short when another girl—the most beautiful girl I've ever seen—strides up to the side of the counter. I can't explain my reaction to her, but my mouth goes dry, and every muscle in my body is suddenly taut with tension.

She's a tiny little thing, short and petite with long blonde hair that falls down her back and around her shoulders in sensuous waves. When she looks up at her friend, her emerald green eyes nearly bowl me over. I feel a warmth settle in my bones as I look into those eyes—though she's not looking at me. They remind me of the rolling green hills of my homeland but even more beautiful.

They're so vibrant and full of life. Shining. She's shining, full of an inner light that seems to tug at me.

Derrick's girl comes around the counter and wraps her in a hug, and I'm instantly jealous. It should be my arms wrapped around her and no one else's.

"Who is that girl?" I ask Derrick slowly, deliberately,

my voice gruff with my sudden need to know her, possess her.

Derrick's eyes take in the look on my face, and he smirks, leaning back to drape an arm over his chair casually. "Oh, just one of Rachel's friends. She comes in here every so often to visit with her. Why?" He blinks at me with wide eyes, the insolent bastard. He knows damn well why. I can't tear my eyes away from her. She's like a little blonde angel, and everything in her is calling to me.

Suddenly, I have a new empathy for Derrick and how he feels about his little barista. If he feels even a fraction of the insane possessiveness I feel for this girl after just laying eyes on her, then I don't know how the hell he hasn't marched over there to claim her for himself yet. From the look on his face, it seems he realizes my plight too, and he's not going to make this easy on me.

I narrow my eyes at him. "So, you're telling me you watch her spend time with your girl and you don't know her name?" I call bullshit. I know Derrick has vetted everyone who comes within a ten-mile radius of his obsession. He knows who the girl is, but like I said, he's not going to make this easy on me after all the ribbing I've been giving him over Rachel.

Instead of answering me, Derrick leans forward, placing his forearms on the table, a devious twinkle in his eyes, "If you want to know her name so badly, why don't you just go ask her."

I firm my jaw and stare back at him. Little does he know I have absolutely every intention of making myself known to her today. I'm not going to pussyfoot around. That's never been my style. When I want something, I go after it. Plain and simple. I'm not really a patient man. I want what I want, and I get what I want.

I smirk back at him before I stand and straighten the lapels of my suit. "Watch and learn, lad."

———

Ella

I swear Rachel is the best friend a girl could ever have. After releasing me from her bone-crushing hug, she turns and grabs a steaming cup of java she already had made for me.

"Thanks, bitch," I tell her affectionately as I grab the cup and take a sip, the taste of sweet, creamy caramel exploding across my tongue.

"Nothing but the best for my bestie," she winks at me as she starts untying her apron. "Seth, I'm off to take my break. Can you handle it?"

Her coworker waves her off absently, and she turns

to me with a grin. "God, let's go sit down. My feet are killing me," she groans dramatically.

"Busy day?" I ask her with a raised eyebrow.

She blows out a breath. "Always." I believe it too. This coffee shop is the hottest one in town. It's always busy no matter when I come in here, but luckily, I never have to stand in line for my cup. Rachel always has mine made ahead of time.

The perks of having a bestie who's a barista.

We turn to start making our way over to a table but are instantly halted by the huge man towering over us.

Scratch that. He's not a man. He's a god.

My head tilts up to look at him, taking in his expensive suit, dark auburn hair, and stylish stubble laid over a finely chiseled jawline. His eyes are a striking shade of blue, and they're staring right down at me like he's trying to see inside me.

He's so much taller than me, though to be fair, it doesn't take much to be taller than me. I've always been a shortie. It's my curse, and it definitely makes reaching the items on the top shelves at the supermarket a pain, but what can you do, right? You gotta work with what you got. Thank god I'm a good climber.

His shoulders are broad, and I just know if I could look underneath that shirt, I'd find washboard abs. The man screams sexy. He looks like he should be on the cover of a fitness magazine. Better yet, GQ or something like that.

He's downright gorgeous.

I blush when I realize I'm staring at him, and his lip tilts up into a crooked grin. "Ladies," he nods at Rachel before his eyes hone back in on me. "I don't believe we've met."

I don't say anything. I'm still staring up at him, taking in the sheer, overwhelming size of him when Rachel luckily chimes in. "No, we haven't. I'm Rachel, and this here is Ella," she nudges me forward, and I shoot her a look.

Oh no, she's got that twinkle in her eyes, and I know exactly what it means. She's going to try to set me up with this guy. Rachel has made no secret of her opinion that it's high time I started dating again. It's been six months since my explosive breakup with my ex-boyfriend, who, consequently, was my first boyfriend. Of course, we'd only been dating for six months when I walked in to find him cheating on me. And to think I'd actually been considering giving the jerk my virginity. So glad I didn't do that. Of course, as it turns out, when I wouldn't put out, he found someone who would.

I wouldn't say I loved him, but the betrayal still ran deep. I swore off all men from that moment on, deciding I would be much happier focusing on my career and living life drama-free.

What's ironic about Rachel always pushing me to get back into the dating field is that she doesn't currently date either. I don't think she's gone out on a date since before I broke up with my ex, so I don't know why she's so adamant about hooking me up with a man. I guess it's because she thinks my heart is broken and wants to fix me, but honestly, it's my pride that's hurt more than anything. Once I was no longer with my ex, I realized that I could live without him, that my life was actually more carefree without him. Sure, we'd gotten along okay while we were together, and while his kisses had been nice, they weren't the toe-curling kisses you read about in books. I'd just assumed that that kind of passion was just fantasy and that real life wasn't like that.

Now I'm just convinced that life is much better without a man period.

"Ella," the god repeats my name with a little smile and a bit of an accent to his voice, and my heart does a summersault in my chest.

What the hell is wrong with me? I've never reacted to a man's presence like this.

It's just because he's so big, I tell myself. *It's intimidating.*

He's gorgeous too, another niggling voice in the back of my head says. *And he has an accent.*

I ignore that voice. That voice is a shameless slut who doesn't know what's good for us.

"I'm Thomas," he introduces himself, and I pinpoint his accent as Irish and nearly swoon. I've always been a sucker for accents.

I take great care to ensure my features stay neutral and impassive. This man is drop-dead gorgeous—and wealthy too by the looks of it. Women are probably falling all over themselves trying to get a chance with him.

He's nothing but trouble. I can already tell.

He still hasn't taken those blazing blue eyes off me. I resist the urge to squirm under the intensity of his gaze. Jesus, why is he looking at me like that?

"Can I buy you a coffee, Ella?"

I hold my cup up in my hand. "Already have one. Thanks." God, I sound like such a bitch, and while part of me grimaces at my tone, the other part of me knows it's necessary because I can't allow this to go anywhere.

I mean, I just can't.

Thomas, the Irish god, isn't deterred, though. He just chuckles, his eyes flicking down to my cup before coming back up to capture my eyes again. And *capture* is the right word because when his gaze grabs mine, it twines around me like a rope, effectively imprisoning me. I can't look away. "So you do. Okay, how about a scone then?"

I shake my head when Ella pipes up, "She loves the raspberry ones."

I shoot a death glare over at my best friend. "I'm not hungry," I counter.

"Then, let me just sit with you and talk," he flashes me a charming smile that I'm sure has many women's knees buckling.

"We were actually fixing to get a table together, right, Rachel?" I glance over at my friend only to see her slinging her apron back on.

"Oh gosh, would you look at the time?" she glances down at her bare wrist. I swear she couldn't be more obvious if she tried. I'm glaring daggers at her. "My break's over. Gotta get back to work!" She gives me a little wink before rushing back behind the counter, effectively abandoning me.

I'm going to kill her. Swear to God, that traitorous bitch...

I turn back around to find Thomas' amused gaze still trained on me. His lips are tilted up into a cocky grin as he comments dryly, "Well, your friend certainly seems to think it's a swell idea for us to get to know one another, so what do you say?"

I take a deep breath to steady myself before I say what needs to be said, "Look, you seem like a nice guy, and it's nothing personal, but I'm just not interested, okay?"

I don't meet his eyes as I deliver my edict. Instead, I turn and begin walking out the door.

It's too awkward to stay in this coffee shop now.

two

. . .

Thomas

I STAND THERE, halfway shocked as I watch Ella leave. The woman just flat turned me down, and I can't remember the last time that happened to me—if it ever has.

I frown, not liking the feeling of rejection.

But I'm not a cad. This isn't about my ego. No, I genuinely *want* this woman. I want her more than I've ever wanted anyone ever before. I don't know what it is about her, but something about her just calls to me. It's more than her pretty face and beautiful body. It's just *her*. I want her, all of her. I want to know every little mundane detail of her life, every thought in that pretty little head of hers.

My god, is this how Derrick feels about his barista? If so, I suddenly have a new empathy for what he's been going through.

Her friend, Derrick's barista, after obviously seeing how Ella shot me down and nearly ran out of the coffee shop, runs over to me and gives me an apologetic smile. "Look, it really isn't you," she tells me. "Ella's just a bit jaded after her ex-boyfriend cheated on her."

"What kind of a fucking moron would cheat on a girl like her?" I growl, pissed off at both the thought of someone hurting her and her being with anyone else.

Rachel nods, agreeing with me. "The thing about Ella is she's stubborn. She sets her mind to something, and she does it, and right now, she's sworn off all men." She shrugs up at me as if that's that, though she doesn't agree with it.

I frown down at her, considering. Well, Ella may have just met her match because I'm as stubborn as they come and persistent as hell when I want something, and what I want is her. And I suspect from the electric current I felt leaping between us like a live wire that she wants me too and is just too afraid to trust again after what her douchebag of an ex put her through. I momentarily entertain myself with thoughts of all the ways I'd like to punch the scumbag for hurting—and touching—my girl.

"How long has she been broken up from this asshole?" I ask, my voice coming out sour. Just the thought of another man's hands on her leaves a bad taste in my mouth.

"Six months," the friend answers, "though honestly she should have dumped him long before he cheated on her. He was always pressuring her to give up her V-card, and then I guess when she kept putting him off, that's why he finally found someone who would..." Her eyes widen, and she claps a hand over her mouth as if she's just realized she's divulged too much of her friend's personal life to an absolute stranger. "Oh my god," she squeezes her eyes shut, "just forget I said all that, okay? Ella will kill me if she knows I let that slip. I don't know what I was thinking."

My mood is already markedly improved when the full weight of what her friend divulged sinks in.

Ella's a virgin. She never slept with her ex-boyfriend. I feel my shoulders relax at the knowledge that no one has ever taken her in that way. And as of this moment, no one ever will. No one besides me, that is. I knew Ella was meant to be mine. Felt it the moment I laid eyes on her.

"Don't worry," I tell the distraught barista. "Your

little slip-up is safe with me." I wink at her, and she sighs in relief.

"Thank you," she gushes.

"If you want to thank me, though," I drag my words out conspiratorially, "you can tell me where I can find your friend," I give her my most charming smile and cock an eyebrow at her.

She studies me for a moment before she smiles back and laughs. "You know what? I think you'd be great for Ella. She needs someone who's willing to go the extra mile to break down all those walls she's built up." She crosses her arms over her chest and eyes me before she grins again. "She owns the yoga studio on eleventh. You can't miss it. It's the only one on the block."

"Thank you, Rachel," I grasp her hand in between mine and give it a gentle squeeze.

I look up to see Derrick glaring daggers at me and release her hand with a smirk. *Easy there, buddy. I'm not interested in your girl.*

I've got one of my own.

————

Thomas

For a moment, all I can do is stand outside the studio and look in at her in awe. She's standing in front of a class, leading them in yoga poses. I watch as her limber little body stretches, my thoughts straying to all the positions I could put that firm little body in while I'm buried balls deep inside her.

I shake my head to get a grip on myself. This girl mesmerizes me. Everything about her from her golden hair to her emerald eyes. God, those eyes. I think those are what captivate me the most. I could just stare into them all day. I could stare at *her* all day.

I vaguely register that my intense fixation on her should probably alarm me. I've never been one of those dopes who believed in love at first sight, but I'll be damned if one look at her wasn't enough to have me obsessed from that moment on.

My eyes rove over her, taking in her tight black yoga pants and pink workout bra. Because that's right. That short little piece of fabric that barely covers her tits doesn't qualify as a shirt. It's a motherfucking bra. I square my jaw and glance around the room at the people in the class, only relaxing marginally when I don't spot any males in attendance. Still, I don't like the fact that any man can be strolling along on the sidewalk out here and look in at her showing off her beautiful body like that. Call me a caveman, but that's just how I feel.

I frown when I think of the ex-boyfriend who hurt her and has her scared to trust any man now.

I square my shoulders and make my way for the door. I'm just going to have to show her that I'm unlike any man she's ever encountered before. I won't pressure her to have sex with me before she's ready, and I'll damn sure never look at another woman when I have her.

I'll be patient. I'll wait for her. I'll go that extra mile to prove how much I want her. I'll beg and grovel if I have to.

But I won't take no for an answer. She's mine. I know it deep down. I feel it in every cell of my body.

And that's non-negotiable.

———

Ella

I know something's up when a couple of the women in my class huddle closer together and begin whispering and giggling to each other and looking up with hearts in their eyes.

I turn around to see what all the commotion's about, my eyes widening in surprise when I see Thomas standing there in all his six-foot, sexy businessman glory.

He smiles that heart-stopping grin of his, and the women behind me practically swoon. He merely nods at them respectfully before turning the full focus of those ocean blue eyes on me.

My lips pull down into a frown to find the man I just turned down at the coffeeshop standing in my yoga studio. "What are you doing here? Did you follow me?"

By way of answer, he merely shrugs, looking completely unapologetic as he says, "All that matters is I found you, right?"

I stare at him for a moment, trying to figure out if he's really as insane as he's coming across before I finally let out an incredulous laugh. "Unbelievable," I mutter as I continue to frown at him, wondering what to do. I can't very well kick him out in front of my customers. That would only arouse even more suspicion and interest than he already has. I usually only get women in here, so the presence of a man—especially a drop-dead gorgeous one like Thomas—has all the women who come here peeking over their shoulders and whispering amongst themselves.

"I just want to talk to you," he asserts, taking a step closer to me.

I scowl and glance over my shoulder at all the eyes on us. Seeing no choice, I finally concede, "We can talk in my office."

I want to kick him when he grins like the Cheshire cat.

He follows so closely behind me I can feel his body heat through our clothing as we step into my office.

He shuts the door behind us, and I step behind my desk to put some distance between us, though I'm not sure what good it does when he walks right up around my desk to stand right in front of me. The man has no concept of personal space, and he clearly can't take a hint when I keep trying to put space between us and he keeps closing it.

The way he's looking down at me, I have a pretty good idea of what he wants to talk to me about, and even though my pulse races at the nearness of his body, the scent of his expensive cologne wrapping around me like a snake, the answer is still no.

I learned my lesson once. I'm not going down that path again.

"What do you want?" I mean for my voice to come out stern, but it comes out as a breathy whisper instead. Damn it

Thomas keeps prowling toward me like a panther stalking a mouse, and I keep taking steps back until the backs of my knees hit my chair, and I'm falling, planting my butt down in the seat.

If the way his eyes gleam are any indication, this is exactly where he wants me.

He places his hands on either side of my desk, framing me in. He leans in so that his face is hovering over me and I feel the minty freshness of his breath fanning over me.

It's a good thing my ass is already sitting down or my knees might have buckled right then.

"You. Me. I want to talk about us, lass." His voice is low and gravelly, his Irish brogue coming out thick and heavy. And oh my god, the way he calls me *lass*.

I press my legs together tightly at the sudden throbbing between them. My god, what his voice alone does to me. I might still be a virgin, but I've read plenty of romance novels, and I can just imagine how that voice would sound right in my ears as he…

I shake my head, snapping myself out of the lust-filled haze his accent momentarily thrust me into.

"There is no us. I don't even know you." Again, I mean to sound strong and firm, but my voice comes out weaker than I'd like.

"So, let's change that. Have a cup of coffee with me."

I shake my head, instinctively turning him down.

He's undeterred. "Dinner then?"

I shake my head again. "No."

He shrugs. "So, a walk in the park?"

I let out an incredulous laugh.

"A movie? Shopping? Skydiving? Hell, a walk around the block?" he tries again, like it's the activity or destination that has me turning him down.

Before I can decline again, he rushes on, his voice sounding half desperate. "I don't really care where we go or what we do, lass. I just want to spend time with ye."

The smoldering look in his blue eyes has me biting my lip and actually considering accepting his proposal.

Those ocean blue eyes hone in on my lips, darkening with desire, and I immediately release the flesh from my teeth.

He drags his gaze back up to my eyes and stares at me intensely. "Please, lass. Give me something here. You're killing me."

I nearly jump out of my skin when my office phone rings behind me. Thomas doesn't budge an inch. He's still got me caged in against my desk and is staring down at me expectantly.

"I've got to take this," I push at him so that I can turn to my desk and grab my phone. Sweet Jesus, when I feel his hard chest under my palms, I nearly swoon.

The man is ripped. I yank my hands off him like I've been burnt and turn to grab my phone.

He reluctantly steps back and allows me to handle my business. One of my regulars has to reschedule her session, but that's okay. My business is popping enough that I'll fill the vacant slot by the end of the day.

The huge Irishman in my office stands patiently by, waiting for me to finish my phone call, the blue flames of his eyes trained on me the entire time.

His thick voice surrounds me the moment I lay the phone back in the cradle. "So, what'll it be, lass? Coffee or dinner or whatever you want. You tell me."

I hesitate. Am I actually considering dating again?

His eyes light up, and a cocky smirk twitches at the corner of his lips as if he senses me relenting.

Before I have a chance to answer, though, there's a knock on my door.

"Come in!" I call out.

A couple of my clients push their way through the door, still whispering and giggling as they do so. They keep glancing over at Thomas and blushing and tittering amongst themselves, and I find myself completely irritated by their behavior.

They claim they just came to remind me that class was supposed to start five minutes ago, but I know they're really only here to try to learn more about this muscled-up businessman in a designer suit that strolled into my yoga studio like he owns the damn place.

Although their transparency annoys me, I'm actually thankful for it because it reminds me of all the reasons I don't want to date again—especially someone who's a woman magnet like the sexy Irishman who's now standing a respectful distance away from me on the other side of my desk as my clients bat their eyelashes at him and assault him with seemingly innocent questions. Never mind that the bitches are both married.

I have to fight to keep from rolling my eyes, especially when Thomas smiles politely back at them and makes small talk with them in that easy way of his.

I force an overly cheery smile of my own. "You're totally right. I'm so sorry to keep the class waiting. We're done here anyway," I refuse to look over at Thomas, though I can feel the intensity of his gaze burning into me at my comment. "I'll meet you on the floor, ladies," I tell them as I practically sprint from my own office, leaving the two women gaping and Thomas scowling behind me.

That was a close call, but I'm actually very glad my clients came in when they did. Otherwise, I might have caved and made a colossal mistake.

three

. . .

Ella

I LET OUT a heavy sigh when I can sense someone come up behind me. I can already smell his unique scent and feel the heat of his body burning my back from where he stands too close to me. Still, I ask Rachel, who's already grinning like a maniac, "Is it him?"

"Oh yeah." She nods her head up and down before she finally laughs.

"See how attuned you are to my body, love?" His voice is right near my ear as he places his hands on my shoulders. "You can sense me. We're tethered together. This pull between us is undeniable." His voice is all dark velvet, and I try to suppress the shiver that runs through me, knowing he'll only use my body's reaction to further his cause. He's been spouting nonsense like this every day for the past two weeks.

I sigh again and turn to face him, pushing his hands off my shoulders and taking a step back out of his reach.

"Or, it could just be that you have no sense of boundaries or personal space and I can just feel you breathing down my neck," I cock my head to the side and give him a fake, sickly sweet smile that's all sarcasm.

As usual, it doesn't put him off. If anything, it merely seems to make his own grin widen. I swear I think he gets off on getting any reaction out of me. He doesn't care if it's negative so long as I acknowledge him.

"Same question, lass," he tells me, his eyes darkening.

"Same answer," I shoot back dryly before I turn my back on him to go back to enjoying my break with Rachel, though why I even bother coming here anymore is beyond me. Thomas has ruined my once-peaceful retreat. I used to come here to catch a few moments with my bestie and have a cup of my favorite midday treat, but every time I come here, he's always here now.

And he asks me the same question every damn day. Will I go out with him?

And I give him the same answer every day. No.

At this point it's more about principle than anything. I've repeatedly told him no, yet he doesn't give up. I think maybe a sadistic part of me is wondering just how many times I have to tell him no before he does.

I feel a pang in my chest at the thought, but then I scoff to myself.

Why the hell would I care if he finally gives up? I mean, that's what I want him to do. I can't get involved in another relationship. I just can't.

No matter how sexy he or his accent is.

Unfazed as always, I hear his deep chuckle from behind me, and I clench my fists and whirl around to face him again. "Just how many times are we going to do this?" I hiss at him. I'm angry, but I think I'm angry at myself more so than I am at him. I'm angry at that little pang I felt when I thought of him finally taking the hint and fucking off. I'm angry for letting him get to me.

He doesn't even bat an eye when he answers back frankly, "Until I get a different answer."

I hear Rachel snicker from behind me, and he shoots her a conspiratorial wink. As if he needs any more encouragement.

I smile at him, and I see his mouth twitching before I ever speak, as if he knows what I'm going to say already.

"Okay, how about this? Fuck off," I say as sweetly as I can.

He laughs a loud, booming laugh that has several people glancing over at us. The man is seriously demented. I tell him to fuck off and instead of doing it, he laughs like it's the funniest shit he's ever heard.

Most guys would have taken a hint by now, but not my Irishman.

I blink as I register my own thoughts. Wait. Hold up. *My* Irishman? Since when the hell did I start thinking of him like *that*? No, no, no, no, no! This is *not* happening! I am not going to let this man continue to get to me like this.

"Let me clarify," he finally says when he gets control of himself again, his blue eyes sparkling. "I'm going to keep asking you until you give me the *right* answer."

I open my mouth to retort something nasty back, but he presses a finger to my lips and prevents me from speaking. I'm so shocked all I can do is stare up at him in a stupor for a moment.

"The right answer is yes, lass." His finger lingers on my lips for a moment before he slides it down ever so slowly. I can still feel the heat from where his finger pressed against my lips. If it's possible for a finger to kiss lips, then consider me thoroughly kissed.

"I'll see you tomorrow then," he winks at me before he turns and begins sauntering his way out the door. The cocky bastard.

I'm still seething and gaping after him like a fish when Rachel's voice breaks into my thoughts.

"Jesus, Ella. That was so hot."

I scowl at her. "A woman telling a guy she's not interested and him refusing to take no for an answer is hot?"

Ella gives me a knowing look. "The chemistry between you two is off the charts, and I think we both know you're interested. You're just too afraid to make that leap of faith."

We take our seats at the table we'd been heading to before a certain stubborn Irishman interrupted us. I take a sip of my macchiato, savoring the rich, caramel flavor on my tongue. "You know why I don't want to date, Rach."

Rachel looks at me with pitying eyes. "Every guy isn't like your ex, Ella. In fact, most of them aren't. You just had the misfortune of picking a loser the first time around."

"Exactly," I say, taking another sip. "I obviously have poor taste in men and aren't a good judge of character. Which is exactly why I shouldn't trust myself to date."

Rachel rolls her eyes at the way I've turned her logic around on her. "Oh, for God's sake, Ella, the man is hot for you! He's been asking you out every day for the past two weeks even though you keep saying no, and he still hasn't given up. A man doesn't put that kind of effort into a woman he doesn't really want."

"Yeah, but," I begin, but she interrupts me.

"For fuck's sake, Ella! Kiss him at least! He's sexy as hell! You've got one of the hottest Irishmen in the city after you and you're running away. At least kiss the poor guy and then see how you feel. If you don't want to get into a serious relationship, then don't, but you could at least have some fun with him." Rachel taps the edge of her untouched coffee cup, pursing her lips as she considers me.

I glance down at my phone and frown when I see the time. Once again, my whole break is gone, and practically every minute of it was spent talking about Thomas or dealing with the Irishman himself. I sigh. "Look, I gotta go, Rach. I've got to give a class in ten."

"Think about what I said, bitch." She cocks a finger at me. "There are worse things than kissing a hot Irishman just to see where it leads."

Yeah, like falling for the Irishman and having him cheat on me.

See, the thing about my ex was I didn't really love him. And if it hurt that much to have someone I didn't love cheat on me, how much more would it hurt to have someone I did love cheat?

And I already know with absolute certainty that Thomas Donovan is the kind of man I could totally fall in love with.

He's dangerous to my heart, body, and sanity, so I just have to keep my distance from him.

***

Thomas

I already know with absolute certainty that I'm in love with Ella Greene. I've never felt this insane obsessiveness before, this primal *need* for a woman. I'm trying my damnedest not to scare her away, though. Yeah, I stalk her like a psychopath and ask her out every day no matter how many times she refuses me, but I try to keep my manner as light as possible. I'm trying to be as patient as I can.

But my patience is running thin.

That's probably why I'm standing outside her yoga studio now in a pair of gym shorts and a black T-shirt. Hell if I know what men wear to do yoga.

My lip twitches as I imagine what Ella's reaction is

going to be when she learns I've booked a private class with her. I had to book it through the receptionist when Ella wasn't here, and she seemed more than eager to accommodate my request.

I don't give two shits about learning yoga, but if this is what it takes to get closer to Ella, then I'm all in. The woman won't give me the time of day otherwise, though I think I'm finally starting to break down her barriers.

Most guys would have given up and moved on by now, but I'm not looking for a quick lay. No, Ella is *mine*. Plain and simple. She was made for me, and I've just got to get her to see that.

For two weeks now, I've watched her—discreetly of course. Ella would have a fit if she knew just how deep my obsession with her runs.

I've learned everything I can about her. I know where she lives. I know her grandfather left her a trust fund and instead of blowing through it recklessly, she wisely started her yoga business. I know she's twenty-one and has only had one boyfriend to date. I frown. That was one too many, but at least the fucker didn't get all the way with her. I know she and the barista my buddy is obsessed with have been friends since grade school. I know she loves peanut butter but hates jelly.

I notice every little thing about her, and it's still not enough. It will never be enough until I can hold her in my arms and be with her all the time and learn *every-thing* there is to know about her. If I could crawl inside her mind and read every thought in there, I would.

I meant what I told her earlier, that I'll keep asking her out every day until she says yes, and maybe me forcing contact with her by enrolling in a private session is pushing the envelope, but I'm dying here.

I've jacked off to images of her in those tight little yoga pants every day since I've met her, but it's all to no avail. As soon as I come, I'm rock hard again at just one thought of her. I have this incessant need that only claiming her as mine will fill. Every time I look at her, my balls get heavy, and my cock aches.

But it's so much more than that. I can endure this physical torture if she'll just let me spend some time with her. I just want to be near her. I'm like a lovesick puppy yearning to follow her around, hoping she'll grace me with one pat on the head.

I *need* to be around my woman.

And she *is* my woman.

Whether she realizes it yet or not.

four

. . .

Ella

I DISMISS my class and head over to the reception area to check my schedule. It's not uncommon for people to book into empty slots at the last minute, and I remember having a cancellation yesterday.

"Mindy, do I have anything scheduled for the next hour?"

She doesn't even look down at the books. "Yep," she grins at me. "He booked your open slot just this morning."

I raise my eyebrows. "He?" Not like I'm gender stereotyping or anything. I think it's great for guys to do yoga. I wish more of them did, actually. I just normally don't get many men through here. My clientele is almost one hundred percent women.

"Yes, he," a deep voice with an Irish brogue rumbles behind me, and I immediately know who it is. I close my eyes and take in a deep breath before I turn around to face him.

Well, I turn around and tilt my head back to look up into his face.

He's smiling down at me like the cat who ate the canary.

"Thomas, what are you doing here?" I ask in exasperation.

"You heard the lady. I'm here for my private yoga session."

I glance back at my receptionist who's regarding us curiously before I step out from behind the counter and walk a few steps away out of earshot. I don't even have to ask Thomas to follow me. He's close on my heels as always.

"I'm excited to get started. I think you'll find me a very eager student." The way he says that is dripping with innuendo, and I feel my cheeks heat, but I don't even dignify that statement with a response.

I scoff and cross my arms over my chest, leveling a look up at him. "*You're* going to do yoga?"

He shrugs and then winks down at me. "Whatever it takes, lass. You won't get a cuppa with me. You won't have dinner with me. I'm at the end of my rope here."

"This is totally inappropriate," I hiss at him.

He raises an eyebrow at me. "How so? Because I'm a man I can't do yoga? That's awfully sexist of you, Ella." He gives me a look of mock hurt.

"What?" I feel my cheeks go even redder. "No, of course not. That's not what I'm implying. It's just…you can't just…" I groan in frustration. Jesus, the last thing I need is for word to get out that I refused to provide a man with a class. That'll kill my business. Plus, were it any other man—one who hasn't been doggedly hounding me to go out with him—we wouldn't even be having this conversation. I'd already be working with him.

So, I square my shoulders and decide to make the most of the situation.

Fine.

If he wants to do yoga, let's do yoga.

Thomas

I smirk in victory when Ella begins leading the way to one of the rooms reserved for private sessions. It's not all out in the open where any passerby off the street can look in like the group classes are. Part of why I booked it.

I can't help admiring her tight little ass in the green yoga pants she's got on today. My hungry gaze devours the skin of her bare back leading up to the black sports bra top.

Oh, she's pissed. I can tell by the ramrod-straight nature of her spine and how she keeps her eyes planted firmly ahead, not once glancing back at me to make sure I'm following her. Granted, I'm sure she's figured out by now I'll gladly follow her anywhere. She doesn't even have to ask.

A fact that's truer than she even knows.

I rub my hands together in anticipation once we reach the private room and are enclosed in the space together. "So, what's first, lass? How about you show me your downward dog?"

She blushes prettily at my request that she show me the pose I quickly realized I love best, as it renders her with her firm ass stuck up in the air. God, what I wouldn't give to come up behind her while she's in that pose…fist my hands in her hair and just go to town until I drive her to continuous orgasm…I'd have her screaming my name and begging for more. I feel my cock twitch in my pants.

My eyes rove over the front of her, taking in the

way her workout top and pants cling to every gentle curve of her trim body.

I've never been one for workout porn, but fuck if Ella doesn't have my mind racing with all kinds of depraved fantasies.

Predictably, she doesn't comment on my request. Instead, she's all business, showing me some basic moves. I play along for the time being, learning the moves. If it'll make her happy, I'll try not to tease her too much. Fuck, I just love seeing how beautiful she looks when her eyes are all lit up and her face is flushed. I'd rather it look like that in the heat of passion, but if all I can get out of her is a rile, then I'll take what I can get.

I quickly catch on to her game when the poses she has me attempting to do become increasingly difficult. I catch her smirking a time or two when she thinks I'm not looking. Every time she sees me looking at her, she's quick to smooth her face into one of impassivity.

I nearly snort. We both know she's anything but impassive. She's pissed, and she's making me pay for my underhanded way of getting her time.

Oh, you're enjoying this, aren't you, lass? Seeing me struggle to get my big body into these ridiculous poses?

A fucker as big as I am just isn't made for this shit. I'm not a goddamned pretzel.

I glance over at her again. Oh, she's taking sadistic

pleasure in her revenge, but that's okay. I don't utter a sound of complaint and give everything she tells me to do my best shot. I've got my eye on the prize.

When looking over at her, though, I lose my balance and fall, smashing onto my knee hard. I grunt. *Fuuuck, that hurt.*

"Oh my god! Are you okay?" Suddenly Ella is rushing over to kneel beside me, her long ponytail brushing against my arm as she drops down next to me. Her sweet scent surrounds me as she bends over to inspect my knee like I'm a kid on the playground who fell.

"I'm fine, lass," I tell her gently, touched by her obvious concern. See? Not as impassive as she'd like me to believe.

I can't help it. I take in a deep inhale, breathing in her intoxicating scent of fresh berries. I'll never be able to sit before a bowl of berries again without devouring the whole bowl, thinking of *her*.

Those beautiful emerald eyes of hers look up at me apologetically. She bites her lip before she says softly. "I'm sorry, Thomas. I shouldn't have pushed you so hard. I knew you weren't ready for those more advanced moves."

I don't ask why she did it because we both already know. She was trying to teach me a lesson, and my lips quirk up at the corners. She's got balls, my woman.

And I really am fine. My knee might just be sore for a day or two, but I've sustained no lasting injury. Still, I can't say it's not nice to have her hovering over me and feeling contrite.

Desperate bastard that I am, I find a way to use the situation to my advantage.

"I know how you can make it up to me." My voice comes out gravelly, and her eyes take on a look of trepidation.

"Thomas…" she begins, no doubt getting ready to turn me down again. She thinks I'm going to try to extort her to go on a date with me again, but she's wrong.

I'm a shrewd businessman, and after employing the same strategy to no avail, I realize when it's time to switch tactics.

"A kiss," I interrupt her.

Her eyes widen, but before she can immediately say no, I rush to add, "One kiss, and if you want nothing to do with me after that, then I'll leave you alone."

She looks at me skeptically. "I give you one kiss, and then you'll leave me alone for good? No more cornering me at the coffee shop every day and asking me out? No more signing up for private yoga sessions?"

I hold up my hand in a boy scout salute. "Scout's honor."

She chews her lips as she hesitates, and I fist my hands together to keep from reaching for her and chewing on that damned lip myself.

Fuck, it's all I can do to keep from pouncing on her. Maybe she's right to be wary of me. I'm like a savage beast ready to devour my prey. The thrill of the chase has only heightened my hunger.

When she's still silent, I know I have to break her from thinking so much. If I let her overthink, she'll find a loophole or talk herself out of it. She's right there on the edge of the cliff, and I need her to take a chance and jump. What she doesn't realize yet is that I'll never let her fall. I'll always be right there to scoop her into my arms where she can soar.

I just need her to give me that chance.

"And plus, it's St. Patrick's Day. Don't you have to kiss me *because* I'm Irish or some shit like that?"

Her eyes shoot up to mine and she finally laughs. "What?" She shakes her head, that ponytail bobbing with the movement. "I don't think that's really a thing. You don't have to kiss someone just because they're Irish and they ask you to."

I nod at her seriously. "I think you do, especially when you've just damn near maimed them and are trying to apologize."

She laughs again, and that sound coming from her

lips causes my chest to tighten. I want to hear her laugh like that every day for the rest of our lives.

When she finally sobers, she purses her lips and then clarifies the terms. "One kiss, and then this is over."

"One kiss," I repeat. I don't repeat the second half of her statement because this—*us*—will never be over. I'm not going to rile her up by telling her that, though.

I'm just bartering for one kiss because I know that's all it's going to take to finally bust through her last barrier and make her mine. And it's not that I'm a cocky son of a bitch. It's just that I know *this*—this thing between us—is right. It goes deeper than either of us can truly fathom, and there's no fighting it. No matter how much Ella is trying to. If I can just get my lips on hers, she'll succumb to me.

I know it.

My blood begins to roar through my veins as I watch her slowly nod her head, agreeing.

This is it. The moment I finally taste what's mine.

five

. . .

Ella

THERE'S a warning bell going off in my head telling me not to do this, that this is a trap. But there's another part of me that's saying this deal is too good to pass up even as yet another part of me gives a pang at the thought of Thomas leaving me alone. Which is ridiculous because I want him to leave me alone.

Right?

That's the only reason I'm agreeing to this one kiss, I mentally reaffirm to myself. Because it'll end this once and for all and I can go back to my boring, drama-free life without a hot and infuriating Irishman dogging me at every turn.

It totally has nothing to do with that other little part of myself that is secretly dying to find out what it would be like to kiss him.

Nope. It's not that at all.

Besides, Thomas didn't specify what type of kiss it had to be—only that it had to be a kiss. I'll quickly press my lips to his in a chaste kiss, and then I'll get right out of here.

That's what I tell myself anyway.

Of course, that's nothing like how it really goes down. I should know by now to never underestimate Thomas or his wiliness.

I lean in ever so slowly to press my lips against his. To his credit, he doesn't move a muscle. He leaves me to take the initiative, letting this be totally my decision, and I find myself very grateful for that. It's like he's totally respecting my actions either way. He's clearly giving me a choice, and that knowledge emboldens me.

I press my lips ever so softly to his, surprised at the burst of pleasure that courses through me once I feel his lips pressed firmly underneath mine.

My hands move up to rest on his hard pecs. Sweet baby Jesus, the chest on this man. I press my lips a bit more firmly to his, savoring the sensation of his surprisingly full flesh against mine, and that's when something in him seems to snap.

Suddenly, a strangled growl rumbles up from his chest. I feel it vibrating against my hands, and then his tongue is insistently parting my lips. He takes full control of the kiss then.

His arms fly around me, hauling me flush against him so I'm straddling his lap, my breasts pressed right against his chest.

I'm so shocked, I gasp, and his tongue takes advantage, sliding right inside my mouth.

And oh my god.

Never, never, never in my life have I experienced anything like this.

The glide of his tongue against mine has wetness instantly pooling between my thighs. I can feel him large and hard, pulsing against me. The man is just as big down there as he is everywhere else.

He growls into my mouth as he tilts my head how he wants me so he can sweep his tongue deeper into my mouth. The way he kisses me is hungry, primal, animalistic.

It has my whole body trembling and melting against him.

And I suddenly can't remember why I've been fighting this.

As if he can sense the direction of my thoughts, he rasps against my lips, "You feel that, lass? You were fuckin' made for me. Why've you been fighting this so much, honey? I know you feel this thing between us. Don't you dare fuckin' deny it." His brogue is coming out thicker in his passion, and god, if it's not turning me on even more.

I don't answer him with words. Instead, I merely whimper and kiss him back, stroking my tongue inside his mouth this time.

I feel his cock jump beneath me. "Fuckin' hell," he growls into my mouth before he takes charge and begins devouring my lips again.

His hands on the bare skin of my back are like hot irons branding me. He begins stroking them up and down me as he continues to kiss me until I feel dizzy.

I don't know what's come over me, but I move on instinct, grinding myself against him, feeling snaps of pleasure shoot through me at the friction.

I gasp at the sensation and throw my head back. He starts kissing and laving on my neck, his hands moving up to cup my breasts through my sports bra.

"Yes, that's it, honey. Rub that sweet thing all over me."

I'd normally be embarrassed, but I'm beyond that point now. All I can think about is how *good* it feels.

Pressure is building deeper and deeper within me, and I begin rubbing against him faster, panting quick little breaths as I feel myself getting closer and closer toward something...something I've never felt before but something I'm suddenly so desperate for I feel like I'll die without it.

His hands finally slip my bra up, and I feel the cool air hit my hard nipples, making them pebble up even more. I jerk and moan when he flicks his thumbs over them, and then I let out a sob when I feel the hot wetness of his mouth envelope one of my hardened buds.

He licks and sucks on my breasts, encouraging me in between with filthy words like "yes, honey," "come all over your man," and "I'm going to lick up all your sweet juices after you cream all over me."

"Thomas!" I gasp out his name as I feel the pressure beginning to bubble over.

"Yes, that's it, lass. Say my name when you come."

He latches off my breast and pulls my ponytail so I'm looking up at him. "Look at me," he demands. "Look in my eyes when you come for me."

I don't know if it's the way he thrusts his hips up at me as he pulls my hair or his words or maybe a combination of the two, but I finally explode.

His blue eyes are twin flames as he watches me come, but I can't hold his gaze for long.

I scream his name as stars burst behind my eyes and I feel the muscles between my legs convulsing frantically, gripping at air as I finally experience my first orgasm.

My whole body goes weak, and I slump against him, burying my head in the crook of his neck.

He holds my trembling body close to him and runs his hands all over my back, stroking me. I feel him pressing kisses against my hairline as he murmurs, "So beautiful when you come, Ella. Mine...all mine..."

I can't even protest his words. Maybe I should, but I don't want to. Because in this moment, I want to believe them so badly.

I am his. I want to be his. Only his.

———

Thomas

When she humped me like a bitch in heat, it was all I could do not to nut all in my shorts. Jesus, she looked so hot riding my cock, and I can't wait to see her doing it when I'm seated deep inside her.

It's still taking everything inside me to hold back now. Every muscle in my body is tense as I try to take deep breaths and calm myself so I don't ravage her like the savage beast inside my body is raging for me to do.

I'm harder than fucking steel, and my balls are heavy and aching, ready to bubble over at any minute.

I can endure the torture, though, if it means I get to

feel her so relaxed in my arms, clinging to me like I'm her lifeline.

As her breathing starts returning to normal, I pull back on her ponytail, seeking out her lips again.

God, she tastes like honey. So sweet and pure. So right. I feel her melt up into my kiss. She twines her tongue with mine, kissing me back, and another surge of victory rushes through me. She's *mine*.

"Ella," I croak out her name, my cock straining in my shorts painfully. I feel a steady stream of precum leaking from the tip and trickling down my shaft. "I need you so fucking much, honey," my voice is desperate, pleading, begging, and I don't give a fuck. I'll do anything she wants—*anything*—if she just lets me have her.

Her eyes search mine for a moment, and I can't help but get lost in the grassy green of her orbs. Those eyes are going to be my undoing. I know it. They're the first thing I want to see every morning when I awaken. They're the last thing I'll see before I leave this earth.

"Don't hurt me," she finally whispers up to me, and my heart wrenches within me. I know she's not talking about the physical act. She's offering me so much more.

Her heart.

"Never," I vow to her, putting more conviction into that one word than I've ever put into anything in my entire life.

She reaches down between us and then peeks up at me almost shyly as she brushes her fingertips across my tip where it's pressing against the elastic of my workout shorts.

"Fuck!" I grit out, that one touch enough to send me spiraling over the edge. A jet of precum shoots from my tip violently, staining the inside of my shorts. I cup the back of her neck and crash my lips to hers again while freeing my erection from its constraints. It jumps out to bob between us, sticking straight up like a proud flagpole.

As much as my cock is dying to find its home inside her, I ignore it for now.

I need to taste her first. Find out if the honey between her legs is just as sweet as her lips.

She gasps when I suddenly lay her out on the floor and shoulder my way between her thighs. My hands are shaking with impatience when I grip the edges of her yoga pants and then pull them and her panties down and off in one fluid motion. Maybe I should go slower, but I'm too wound up.

I'm panting with need by the time I finally have her spread bare before me, and motherfuck. Her folds are glistening with juices. I inhale deeply, marveling at how she even smells sweet.

Her legs are trembling when I finally dive into her, licking and sucking and tasting the sweet nectar between her thighs.

She shudders and gasps beneath my hold, especially when I find her little nub and begin to pay it special attention.

I thrust my tongue into her hole, feeling how tightly it grips my tongue. Fuck, I don't know how I'm going to get my cock one inch in her without busting. She's the tightest thing I've ever felt.

I go back to licking her clit and replace my tongue with one finger. I carefully press it into her. She whimpers at the invasion and buries her fingers in my hair. I increase the pressure of my tongue on her clit and am rewarded with renewed wetness, allowing my finger to slide deeper inside her. I begin to add another finger, stretching her as gently as I can.

Sweat breaks out on my brow, and I can't sit still. I'm humping air, my staff straining and bobbing wildly, wanting to get to her.

I increase my ministrations, circling my tongue around her bundle of nerves and sucking insistently while I stroke my fingers in and out of her. I feel her tightening underneath me, and I look up at her, wanting to see her as she falls apart.

She's whimpering incoherent nonsense. "Thomas, please…don't…no…yes…oh my god!"

Her juices soak my fingers as she comes, her greedy

pussy sucking on the digits still buried inside her. My cock goes mad with jealousy.

Fuck it, I *need* to be inside her. *Now.*

I move on top of her, lining myself up against her sopping wet hole, pushing just the head in.

My eyes damn near roll back in my head at the sensation of her tight heat just around my tip.

I brace myself on my elbows and look into her eyes. "Tell me you're mine," I order her.

Her green eyes snap up to me, and I wonder for a moment if she's going to fight me on this.

But she doesn't. Her eyes seem to heat as she breathes, "I'm yours, Thomas."

I groan and push into her, feeling her tense as I reach her hymen.

"Relax, lass. Just let me in." I'm panting like a wild beast. My balls are already churning, and I'm not even halfway into her. *Jesus Christ.*

I begin licking her lips gently until I feel her soften beneath me. While still distracting her with my mouth, I thrust hard and deep, breaking through her barrier and seating myself completely inside her.

She screams, but I capture her cry with my lips. I fight every instinct in my body that's telling me to move and hold still inside her, letting her become accustomed to me. I also need the moment of stillness to keep me from ejaculating prematurely like a some horny teenager getting his dick wet for the first time.

Christ Almighty, nothing could have prepared me for the feel of her. She's nirvana. If there is indeed a heaven, it's right here in between her thighs. Everyone else can go to hell, though, because my cock is the only one that will ever be nestled inside her like this.

I continue to kiss her until I feel her softening beneath me again. When her muscles contract and grip me tightly, a shudder passes through me, and I curse into her mouth, pulling out slightly and jabbing back into her instinctively.

She gasps into my mouth, and I finally release her lips long enough to praise her, "Look at how good you're doing, lass. Taking my big cock so perfectly." I begin to move in and out of her fast, groaning at the intense pleasure lighting up my entire being.

I tilt her face up, needing to look into her eyes, "This is more than just sex, lass. You hear me? Feel this?" I stroke in and out of her slowly. "This is us. You and me. Forever. You're mine now. No more fighting this. I know you feel it too."

She moans and nods her head in assent before she lifts her hips, fucking me back.

I lose sight of all my senses then. Knowing that she wants this just as badly as I do, feeling her throwing her sweet little pussy up at me, it's enough to send me spiraling off the edge of sanity.

I grip the side of her thigh as I begin hammering up into her. Her arms and legs wind around me as she clings to me and holds on.

I can't speak now. I'm huffing and puffing and grunting as I mate her hard and rough, primitively.

God, I meant to go slow and gentle with her, but I can't help myself. I can't control myself now.

My balls are tightening, and I'm lengthening, my shaft swelling in preparation for the eruption that's fixing to take place.

"Thomas!" she moans my name loudly, her back arching, her body vibrating. She's wound up tighter than a bowstring, and I stab inside her again, plucking her one last time, needing to feel her fall over the cliff with me.

"Come for me lass," I growl out.

She screams as she spasms around me, her tight muscles milking me for all I'm worth.

"Fuck, Ella!" I roar as I feel my cum racing up my length. I damn near collapse in pleasure when I feel the first jets shooting from my tip. I'm jerking inside her while she quakes all around me, and I swear to God, I've never felt anything more intense in my whole motherfucking life.

I don't know how long I continue to spill inside her,

but by the time my balls are drained and I slump life-lessly, barely holding myself up above her, I know one thing for certain.

My obsession for this girl before was nothing. Now that I've been inside her and made her mine, *obsession* doesn't even begin to cover the insane possessiveness and protectiveness vibrating throughout my entire being for her.

I can never be without her again. I'll go insane. I'll die.

She's going to have to get used to it. There are no second thoughts or going back now. Ella is finally and truly mine. In every way.

six

. . .

Ella

THOMAS FLIPS us so that I'm laying atop him. He wraps his arms around me and holds me close to his chest. I can feel his heart beating in tandem with mine, and I marvel at how great it feels to be completely wrapped up in him like this. His body is so hard underneath mine, yet I'm completely comfortable. I can see myself slipping off to sleep on him just like this with my head pressed against him, listening to his heartbeat lull me to sleep like the best lullaby.

We just lay there like that in silence for a few moments, enjoying the other's heat. We don't speak. No words are needed to convey what's already been said with our bodies.

My lips finally tilt up into a wicked grin as a thought comes to me. I give Thomas' arm a tiny pinch and feel him jerk beneath me.

"Ow!" he feigns more hurt than I know he feels, rubbing at the spot I pinched. "What was that for, lass?"

I shrug and look up at him from where I'm still sprawled atop him. "You're not wearing green, and seeing as how you're *so* bent on keeping with St. Patty's Day traditions…"

He throws his head back and laughs, the sound vibrating through me. "Touche, love," he grins, obviously still amused as he grabs my neck and kisses me again.

I kiss him back lazily, feeling more content than I can ever remember feeling. The way this man is looking at me and holding me like I'm the most precious thing in his world has me wondering why I was ever afraid of giving in to him.

He's not my ex. Look at how long he chased me, at how far he was willing to go to be with me.

I start giggling and pull away from him.

"Okay," he says, "that's not usually the reaction a man's hoping to hear when he's kissing his girl. What's so funny, lass?" He's lips are tilted up as he regards me good-naturedly, not truly upset in the least.

"I can't believe you did yoga for me."

His grin widens. "I told you I'd do whatever it took. Apparently, yoga is what it took. Or rather, injuring myself so that you felt bad enough to kiss me." He winks at me, and I flush.

I tilt my head up to eye him suspiciously. "Wait, you didn't plan your injury, did you?" I wouldn't put it past him.

He laughs. "No, lass. I didn't purposefully fall on my ass in front of you. You were just too damn distracting in those tight little pants and that bra."

I raise my eyebrow at him. "So you saw an opportunity and then took advantage of the situation."

"Unapologetically," he agrees with a smug grin.

"Aren't you concerned that I might have only kissed you out of pity?" I blink up at him innocently.

His grin only widens. "Not in the slightest because that pity kiss led to the single most incredible experience of my life."

I blush at his frankness, undeniably pleased that he's so pleased with me.

"Oh shit," I hurry to scramble off him when I realize that I've lost track of the time.

"What is it?" he sits up on his elbows, frowning up at me.

I barely have time to admire the way his muscles

ripple with every move he makes as I hurry to put my pants back on.

"What time is it?" I ask him.

I see his eyes flick to the clock stationed on the wall behind me. I could have turned and checked it myself, but I'm busy trying to reassemble myself so it's not obvious I just lost my virginity right here on the studio floor.

"Almost the top of the hour," he answers before he stands and starts getting dressed himself. "You have a class."

He doesn't ask it like a question. He states it like he already knows, and well, I guess he does seeing as how the man seems to know my entire freaking schedule better than I do.

When I'm dressed, I stand there uncertainly, suddenly feeling awkward and not sure what to say to him. Crazy how I felt more at ease with him when I was naked in his arms.

He doesn't allow me much time to feel that way, though, because he pulls me to him and lopes his arm around my back. "There aren't any men in this upcoming class, are there?" His lips are pressed into a thin line, and I gape at him as I realize he's jealous.

I shake my head, a little smile playing on my lips. "No, you're the only male I've had come through here in a while."

"Good," he growls. "I'm the only man you're allowed to do yoga with from now on. New policy."

I raise an eyebrow at him. "You can't just start making demands like that. If a guy does walk in here wanting to do yoga, you know yourself I can't turn him away based on his sex alone. That's discrimination." I throw his own game back at him, for that's exactly what he'd done earlier to ensure I had to work with him.

He scowls before he says close to my ear, "Trust me, lass, if you don't want a murder on your conscience, you'll find a way to tactfully decline any motherfucker with a cock who wants to book a class with you. It's bad enough I have to deal with them ogling you from the street in that little top." He fingers the hem of said top before he goes on, "There's no way in hell I'm going to tolerate another man being in the room with you when you're dressed like this."

I should be horrified at his implication, and a part of me is, I suppose, but a shiver of desire also runs up my spine at the possessiveness in his words and the gravelly grate to his voice as he breathes them right against my ear.

"I've got to go," I finally manage to say when I find my own voice. "My class is starting in five."

I step back from him to leave, but he suddenly

grabs me and whirls me back to him, planting his lips on mine in a fierce kiss that leaves me breathless and shaky.

"Remember who you belong to, lass." He kisses me again, more softly this time, his lips lingering over mine for a moment as we just breathe in each other's breaths.

Good lord, if he wanted to, he could take me again right now and I wouldn't breathe a word of protest.

As if sensing that but knowing that I have to get back to work, he steps back from me, a smirk on his gorgeous lips.

I shake my head to snap myself out of the trance the man seems to have put me in.

One kiss. That's all it took for him to smash through every protective shield I put up after my ex.

But seeing the way his blue eyes are regarding me as if I'm life itself, I can't find it in myself to regret it.

———

Thomas

"You can't be serious?" she's gaping at me like I've just sprouted two heads. I firm my jaw.

"Deathly," I reply seriously. This is non-negotiable.

She's moving in with me. I can't be apart from her now. I just *can't*.

"Thomas, I can't just move in with you just like that," she shakes her head and bites her lower lip.

"You can and you will," I say stoically.

She opens her mouth like she's going to protest, but I interrupt her with a finger on her lips. I pull her tight little body against mine, my cock already responding to the feeling of her against me. Another minute and I'll be fully hard. That's what she does to me.

"You're mine, Ella," I remind her firmly. "You said so yourself. You gave yourself to me. There's no going back from that. You hear me, lass?"

"But," she begins. I'm having none of that, though. Panic flares in my chest at the thought of her not coming home with me. I crash my lips down onto hers, effectively silencing her.

She immediately melts against me and starts kissing me back. I fight off the grin pulling at my lips. She can fight it all she wants, but her body knows she's mine.

When she finally manages to extricate herself from my gasp, she stands there with swollen lips, looking up at me dazedly.

God, if I don't want to kiss her again.

Before I can lean in to follow through on those

intentions, she takes another step back from me, like she already knows what I've got planned.

"What about all my stuff? I need clothes, and everything is at my apartment. It would just be easier if I keep staying there for a while." The hopeful expression on her face irritates me. Is the thought of staying with me so abhorrent to her?

"No!" She jumps when my voice comes out as a bark, and I work to gentle it before I speak again. "I'll send someone to collect your things. That's not an issue. What *is* an issue is why you're fighting me on this. You're mine. I'm yours. We're staying together. It's that simple, Ella."

Her little brow is furrowed, and she's worrying that damn lip between her perfect teeth to death. I capture her in my arms again and tilt her head until I can look directly into her emerald green eyes.

"I can't be without you, Ella. Not now. We've already wasted so much time. I don't want to be apart for another night. Please just give me this. I'm going to take care of you," I promise her. "I'm never going to hurt you. You have nothing to be afraid of with me, honey." I swear to God, if I can ever get my hands on the motherfucker who put such suspicion and trepidation in my little angel's eyes, I'll annihilate him.

Her eyes soften at my words, and she finally nods, blushing shyly. "Okay."

Joy crashes through my chest at her acceptance.

I'm finally going to take my girl home.

With me.

Where she belongs.

seven

. . .

Ella

I CAN'T STOP SMILING. I've been living with Thomas for a week now, and it's so much more amazing than I ever imagined living with a man could be. My nights are no longer spent lonely. I wake up to find him already awake and staring at me while I sleep, and I fall asleep in his arms after he thoroughly takes me every night. Sometimes he fucks me. Sometimes, we make love. That first night when he took me home, he showed me the difference between being fucked and being made love to. Admittedly, I love both, but there's just something so intimate about the way he loves me slowly, kissing every inch of my body and looking into my eyes the whole time until our passion crashes over us in waves. The release is no less intense than it is when he loses control and takes me hard and rough. In fact, it may be even more so simply because of the soul-deep connection we share during those moments.

I shiver now as I remember his whispers on my skin, words of possession and love. While he hasn't come right out and said those three little words yet, he might as well have. His eyes say it every time he looks at me, and I can't help basking in the warmth I find there.

If there is only one negative to being with him like this, it's that I don't get as much sleep as I used to. Still, I'll never chalk that up to a negative because the trade-off is so worth it. He keeps me up late giving me orgasm after orgasm until I pass out on his chest. No, that's not a figure of speech either. I literally fall asleep on the man's chest when he's holding me after making me come four or five times a night.

Despite my lack of sleep, I don't have bags under my eyes, nor do I feel or look tired. On the contrary, I must be practically glowing like a pregnant woman or something because *everyone* seems to note the change in me. My customers keep cocking their heads to the side and telling me that I look great. What did I do different? I just smile and shrug because I certainly can't tell them that I'm being fucked three ways to Sunday by the hottest Irishman to ever come out of Ireland.

If there's one person who knows the reason and comments on it, it's my best friend, Rachel.

"Damn, I swear getting dicked down every night is doing wonders for you. Maybe I need to find me a hot Irishman myself," Rachel wiggles her eyebrows at me.

I swat at her and hiss, "Rachel, keep your voice down. People can hear you."

She shrugs, obviously unconcerned. "So what? If I had a hot guy like Thomas locked down, I'd be announcing it to the world. You do realize just how hot the man you're banging is, right?"

I shake my head at her, though I can't stop the smile that curves up at the corners of my lips. I mean, she's not wrong. "Yes," I admit. "I do realize how hot he is."

"Well, I'm glad to hear that," Thomas' deep voice rumbles in my hair as I feel his arms encircle me from behind.

I relax back into him, instantly calmed by his presence, though I berate him for eavesdropping, "You shouldn't be listening in on conversations about yourself."

He smooths my hair back over my shoulder and kisses the shell of my ear. "How else am I going to find out what my woman really thinks of me?" A delicious shiver runs up my spine at the sensation of his lips on that sensitive spot. I tilt my head back to look up at him and find him smirking.

He knows exactly what he's doing to me.

"Stalker," I throw at him playfully as I narrow my eyes at him, though I really don't think that accusation is too far off. He did pretty much stalk me after we first met, dogging me at every turn, trying to convince me to give him a chance.

I'm secretly very glad now he didn't give up.

"Only with you," he whispers into my ear before he finally kisses my lips and then straightens. He nods over at Rachel who is watching us with a slack-jawed look on her face. "I swear you two are too cute together," she says while fanning herself.

Thomas smirks while I blush scarlet. I've never been big on public displays of affection, but I always forget where I'm at when Thomas is near. He could lean me over this table right now and fuck me senseless, and I'd let him.

"Okay, I gotta get back behind the counter. You guys want something?" Rachel stands and glances down at us. She was already on her break when I walked in, so rather than wasting time to stand in line to order, I just sat down with her, figuring I'd place my order afterward.

"Oh, I want an Irish cream latte," I tell her.

Thomas' lips are suddenly right against my ear again as he darn-near growls, "I've got your Irish cream right here for you, lass."

I smash my legs together under the table to try to ease the sudden ache that's bloomed between my legs. My face goes beet red, and Rachel is regarding me curiously, a wicked smile on her face as she no doubt guesses at the kind of filth he just whispered in my ear. "What about you, Thomas?" she asks him.

"Americano, black," he winks at her and then takes the seat she vacated when she scurries off to make our cups.

"What happened to your usual caramel macchiato?" he asks me. I can't help admiring how his broad shoulders flex under his business suit as he places his hands on the table. Of course, now I'm staring at his hands. God, I love his hands. They're so big and strong and beautiful, and I remember how they felt on me last night when we were...

I look back up to find amusement in his light blue eyes like he knows where my thoughts were going.

I shrug and decide to throw his own game back at him. "I don't know. I've just been craving Irish cream lately. Must have something to do with the man I'm living with."

He cocks an eyebrow at me as his lip twitches. "Is

the Irish cream he provides you with not to your satisfaction, lass?"

I shrug again before tilting my head and commenting coyly, "Oh, it's good. It's just not enough."

His eyes darken, and he leans over the table closer to me. "You telling me I don't fuck you enough, lass? That can easily be remedied."

I bite my lip, and his eyes flick down to them. He barely suppresses a groan as Rachel walks over and places our cups on the table. "Enjoy!" she spouts off cheerily before she heads back behind the counter.

I take a sip of my brew and close my eyes, savoring the creamy richness. When I open them, it's to find Thomas' dark gaze still pinned on me. "How is it, lass?"

I smile at him. "The best Irish cream I've ever tasted." I don't know why I keep goading him. Maybe because it's fun to see him being the one all flustered for a change. Usually, he's the one riling me up and teasing me.

His lips press into a thin line, and his nostrils flare before he suddenly grabs my hand and pulls me up, leading me quickly to the back of the coffee shop where the restrooms are located.

"Thomas!" I hiss at him. "What the fuck—"

I never get to finish my question because the next thing I know, he's pulled us into one of the vacant back rooms. It's not a bathroom. It looks more like a broom closet or something, but I hardly have time to register that before he slams me against the door and lifts me in his arms, his lips crashing down onto mine as he kisses me hungrily.

"Did you really think you could get away with teasing me like that, lass, and I wouldn't fuck you?" he rasps against my mouth as he works to pull my pants and panties down to my ankles.

"Thomas, we can't do this here," I try to tell him, mortified at the thought of someone walking in on us. "What if someone sees?"

"Then let them eat their hearts out when they see the only man who's ever going to have you balls deep inside that sweet little cunt." He undoes the fly of his pants, and his swollen flesh pops free. I see moisture already beading at the tip, and I feel an answering rush of wetness pooling between my thighs.

His fingers move down to test my readiness, and he groans when he feels how wet I am. "That sweet little thing is weeping for my cock, honey."

He positions himself at my entrance and enters me in one swift thrust, and I completely forget where we are. All I can think about now is him and how completely he fills me.

I can't stop the cry that leaves my lips, but he covers my mouth with his hand to silence me. "You wanted some Irish cream, honey. You got it. And don't you for a minute try to tell me mine isn't the best Irish cream you've ever tasted." He growls the words out in between pants as he thrusts up into me hard and furious, going deeper than I think he's ever gone before. He always feels bigger in this position, and my eyes roll back in my head as I feel myself getting ready to come already.

"That's it, honey," he encourages me. "Cream all over your man's big dick."

He covers my mouth in a greedy kiss as I scream into his mouth. I'm quaking all over him as release floods my entire being.

I feel him swelling inside me and know he's close too. Instead of coming inside me like he normally does, he suddenly pulls out, directing me to my knees.

I obey him without question, instinctively taking him into my mouth, already knowing what he wants.

I taste myself on him, and all it takes is one hard suck and one swirl of my tongue along the underside of his tip before he's fisting his hands in my hair and cursing, his brogue thicker than ever, as he comes in my mouth.

I suck down his salty essence, savoring the taste of him mixed with my own juices still gleaming on his staff.

His thighs are trembling underneath my palms where I'm gripping onto him to steady myself, and it fills me with a rush of power to know that I can make this big, powerful man lose control like this.

"Ella," he drops to his knees before me and pulls me into his arms. "Jesus, honey, you make me lose my damn mind."

"I was wrong," I breathe into his neck.

He pulls back to look down at me with a puzzled frown.

"Yours really is the best Irish cream I've ever tasted," I admit.

He laughs, amusement lighting up his eyes. "It better be the only Irish cream—or any cream—you ever taste from a man." His eyes darken a bit at his last statement. If I've learned one thing about Thomas in the week that I've been living with him, it's that he's fiercely possessive of me. He doesn't even like to think of me being with another man and glares at anyone who stares at me a bit too long. He insists on dropping me off at work and picking me up every evening, and I think he'd even make it so I have to wait for him to take all my breaks if the coffee shop wasn't just a few blocks down my studio and he didn't know I would balk at not ever getting any girl time with my bestie. If Thomas could have me permanently attached to him at the hip, I think he would.

It's intense how much he wants me, and while it can be overwhelming at times, I won't lie and say that I don't eat up the attention. I like knowing that he's so obsessed with me. It means I don't have to worry about him ever entertaining thoughts of anyone else.

And I need him to know the same about me, that he's all I think about too.

I lean up and kiss him softly, wordlessly reassuring him that he's the only man I'll ever want.

He relaxes again and kisses me back, and I melt against him like I always do.

I still haven't remembered that we're in a damn broom closet until he finally helps me to my feet and redresses me.

I guess now I know better than to make jokes about Irish cream...

eight

. . .

Ella

I'M ACTUALLY HUMMING to myself as I head toward the coffee shop. I'm going to have more time than usual to catch up with Rachel now that one of my privates canceled on me. That's totally okay, though, because I honestly need the break. Thomas kept me up even later than usual last night, intent on wearing me out and making me eat my implication that he doesn't fuck me enough.

I'm still deliciously sore. I'll never make that mistake again.

Then again, maybe I will...

I fight back a smile so I don't look like a fool

walking down the street by myself with a goofy grin on my face.

I consider swinging by Thomas' office instead of going to the coffee shop, but then I remember that he has a meeting today. Plus, I've never been to his office before, so I'm not sure how cool it would be for me to just pop in—never mind the fact that the man has been showing up at my place of business since before we were technically dating or living together or whatever you call us. We've never really discussed any labels other than I'm *his*.

The sidewalks are busy with plenty of people hurrying along. It's around lunchtime, so there's plenty of hustle and bustle. Someone bumps into me and jostles me toward the window of a restaurant. It's one of those fancier places I've never eaten in, but I've heard the food is to die for.

I know Thomas will take me there if I express any interest in going, and I make a note to drop a hint about it tonight.

I'm fighting another stupid grin at the thought of my sexy Irishman when I look up, and it's like ice has been dumped on my head.

My smile fades completely, and I feel tears prick my eyes at what I see through the window.

It's Thomas looking as handsome as ever, but he's not alone.

A breathtakingly gorgeous woman with red hair sits across from him. She throws her head back and laughs, and he smiles at her indulgently. My heart breaks into a million pieces when I note the familiarity between them.

They seem to know each other well—*very* well.

The final crack completely shatters my heart when they stand and I watch her lean up like she's going to kiss him.

I spin and take off running down the sidewalk. I can't witness his betrayal. It was bad enough watching a man I didn't love screwing another woman, but I absolutely cannot watch Thomas kiss another woman. Somehow, that's way worse than seeing my ex's dick in some whore. Maybe it's because in the short amount of time since I've known Thomas I've fallen completely and totally in love with him.

Stupid, stupid, stupid little fool! I mentally berate myself. I knew better! I fucking knew better! This right here is exactly why I swore off men. I think of the sneaky way Thomas phrased his "meeting." He never specified that it was a business meeting. My dumb ass just assumed that it was. I never imagined it was a rendezvous with another woman.

I'm hurt and more than a little confused. Why the hell does he act so possessive of me if he's involved with another woman? Why did he put so much effort into getting me to be with him if he was going to have someone else on the side?

My stomach plummets, and I feel like I'm going to be physically ill when another possibility hits me. Oh my god, am *I* the other woman?

Of course, I am. He looks so perfect with that redhead. They certainly looked better together than me and him do. She was just as polished and fancy looking as he is. She definitely doesn't traipse around in yoga pants and sportswear all day long.

What was I? Just a challenge? Forbidden fruit that he only wanted because I'd said no? Is Thomas one of those guys who wants to have his cake and eat it too?

My heart is screaming at me not to believe it, that I know Thomas, that we have a soul-deep connection, but my eyes and mind can't forget what they saw.

I'm running into people and getting a ton of dirty glances and stares, but I don't care. Tears are streaming down my cheeks full force now, but I don't stop running until I'm inside my apartment.

There's no way in hell I'm going back to Thomas' place. I don't know how I'm going to get all my things. I can't even think about that now. I barely manage to get it together long enough to call the studio and have my receptionist cancel the rest of my day.

Thomas' betrayal has completely wrecked me. I can't function right now.

I fall to the floor and curl up into a ball, sobs wracking my body at the pain that's tearing through me.

I thought being cheated on hurt the first time around, but it's nothing—*nothing*—compared to this.

———

Thomas

I accept Gwen's kiss on the cheek and hug her back. "Thanks for all your help, sis."

"I can't wait to meet her!" she squeals back at me, practically dancing on her tip toes in delight. My sister has always wanted a sister, and she knows how serious I am about Ella now. It's going to be all I can do to keep her from spilling the beans to my girl prematurely once she meets her.

"I want it as soon as possible," I remind her.

"And I want to meet her asap—tonight," she gushes back at me.

I frown down at her. She never was one for keeping secrets. "I swear to god, Gwen, if you slip up and say anything to Ella before I get a chance to—"

She cuts me off with an eyeroll. "For Christ's sake, Thomas, I was eight years old when I told everyone you had a crush on Katie McAllister. I tell one secret of yours, and you're never going to let me live it down. I'm not a child anymore. I'm perfectly capable of keeping secrets."

I glance down at my watch. It's almost time for Ella to be heading to the coffee shop.

"Gotta go, Gwen. Keep me updated." I hug her one last time.

"Call me about tonight! We can all do dinner!" she calls after me, as relentless as usual when she wants something. I shake my head with a smile and a backwards wave.

I pick up my pace, eager to see my woman, but I frown when I get there and don't see her blonde head anywhere.

My frown only deepens when I speak to Rachel, who tells me that Ella hasn't been in here at all today and that she's never been late to one of their coffee breaks.

I try to call her, and panic begins setting in when her phone goes straight to voicemail.

I hurry up the street to her studio where her receptionist tells me that she left an hour ago and that she ended up calling in and telling her to cancel all the rest of her classes for the day.

Worry begins knawing at me, and I try her cell phone again. Straight to voicemail.

This is all unlike her, and an unsettling feeling steals over me.

"I hope everything's okay," her receptionist says, looking up at me with concerned eyes. I mutter something back to her, but my mind is in a fog. I don't even know what I say to her.

I can hardly see past the fear that's suddenly gripping me at not knowing where my girl is or if she's safe.

I grip my phone tightly in my hand and hurry back home, praying to god that she's there and that everything's okay.

Unsurprisingly, my penthouse is empty. I roar with rage and pull at my hair, furious at the feeling of helplessness that overtakes me. Where the fuck is she?

My chest is heaving as I stand there damn near hyperventilating, imagining every horrible scenario my mind can conjure up. Did someone take her? Is someone trying to hurt her? Did she suddenly start having second thoughts and leave me?

I firm my jaw. I can't believe she'd do that. This thing between us is too real. I know she feels it too. She damn near melts every time I look at her or touch her.

Still, I decide to try to go about this rationally and head off to check her apartment first before I jump to any more conclusions.

Please, God, let me find her...let her be okay...

nine

. . .

Ella

A KNOCK SOUNDS at my door, and I ignore it at first. I don't want to see anyone, least of all Thomas, and he's the only person I can think of who would be beating on my door that way.

When the knocking only becomes more insistent, I finally pull myself up off the floor and stomp over to the door in a flurry, ready to give the asshole a piece of my mind.

I fling the door open and halt when I see that it's not Thomas beating down my door like a maniac.

It's my ex.

Tim.

Oh my god, I am so not in the mood for this. My bad mood just tripled, and I grab the door to slam it in his face, but he sticks his foot out and shoulders his way in, preventing me from shutting him out.

"Ella, just hear me out. I just want to talk to you. I saw you flying down the street, and I just wanted to make sure you're okay." He's just as blonde and athletic and good-looking as I remember, but his beauty pales in comparison to Thomas'. My heart wrenches within me as I think of my Irishman's dark auburn hair and light blue eyes that blaze down at me with such possessiveness.

I scowl at myself. Obviously, that had all been fake. And he's not *my* Irishman. He never really was. I'm just a stupid, stupid, girl who opened herself up to getting hurt again against her better judgement.

I shake my head, trying to rid his image from my mind and focus my attention on the nuisance in front of me. I almost laugh out loud at the concerned look in his eyes. Where was that consideration for me and my feelings six months ago when he was boning another chick because I wouldn't give it up to him?

"I'm fine," I spit at him as I try to shut the door again. Again, he keeps me from shutting it by standing half in my doorway. I huff up at him. "Why the hell do you care anyway? Shouldn't you be with," I wave my hand in the air, "what's the name of that chick you were fucking again?"

Tim grimaces at the reminder of his indiscretion. "She's long gone, Ella, and she never meant anything to me. That was just something that happened in a moment of weakness. I swear it. I never meant to hurt you. I miss you, Ella." He reaches out and takes my hand, trying to pull me closer to him.

I don't even get a chance to protest and tell him to let me go before an inhuman roar echoes down the hallway and he's suddenly being wrenched back from me.

I gasp as I look up and see Thomas furious and practically foaming at the mouth as he holds Tim up by his collar like he's a sack of potatoes.

"What the fuck man?!" Tim screams. "Who the fuck are you?"

Thomas snarls at him, "The boyfriend. Who the fuck are you, and why are your hands on my woman?"

"Thomas, stop!" I scream at him, both confused and frustrated by him claiming to be my boyfriend, finally putting a label on us when I just caught him getting cozy with another woman. "He's just my ex. Put him down." I'm suddenly afraid for Tim as Thomas continues to growl at him like he's going to eat him for breakfast. I used to think Tim was big and muscular, but he's a shrimp compared to Thomas. Not that I particularly care one way or the other what happens to Tim, but I don't want him to end up dying on my account.

Apparently telling Thomas he's my ex was the wrong thing to say, though, because he turns a menacing glare back toward Tim, who's still dangling by his shirt collar.

Thomas' lips curl up into a sinister smile as he says, "I've been fantasizing about what I'd do to you if I ever got my hands on you, lad."

Tim looks flustered. "What the fuck did I ever do to you, man?" he holds his hands up in supplication, no doubt knowing when he's out of his league.

Thomas doesn't answer right away. Swift as lightning, he rears back and punches Tim straight in the nose.

My hands fly up to cover my mouth. I'm too shocked to scream or protest or do anything.

"Fuck!" Tim screams as Thomas finally releases him, shaking the hand he hit my ex-boyfriend with. Tim drops to the floor, writhing in pain.

"That's for hurting her," Thomas spits down at him, his voice full of venom. "Now get the fuck out of here before I break every one of your ribs too, and don't you ever lay another finger on her again. Don't even fucking breathe in her direction. If I find you anywhere near her, I'll fucking destroy you. Do you understand me?" Thomas' voice is vibrating with barely suppressed anger, and Tim stumbles up and scurries off without another word or a backward glance at me.

Only when he's gone does Thomas turn those furious eyes down on me, only there's concern there too.

"Did he hurt you?" his voice comes out rough and thick. His brogue is always thicker when he's on the verge of losing control.

"Why do you care?" I cry at him, my tears suddenly coming hot and fast again.

Thomas looks down at me in bewilderment, his brow furrowed. "What do you mean why do I care, lass? I care about everything about you. You're mine, and I'll be damned if I let another man touch you—much less hurt you."

"Stop saying that!" I scream up at him, my hair flying around my shoulders as I snap my head up to glare at him angrily. I'm well aware that I must look like a mess with tangled strands sticking to my face, my eyes red and swollen.

Thomas frowns down at me, looking more confused than ever. "You're going to have to catch me up here, lass. I seem to have missed something. Why are you upset with me?" His jaw suddenly hardens, and his gaze turns icy as he asks me, "You didn't want him touching you, did you? Are you considering getting back together with that fucker?"

I can't answer at first. I'm so stunned by his completely wrong assumption.

"Over my dead body," he growls when I don't answer, grabbing me by the shoulders.

"Why do you care?" I finally manage to get out. "I saw you with her."

When he just stares at me dumbly, I elaborate, "At the restaurant."

His eyes light with recognition, and he seems to relax somewhat, though why the fuck he would relax at being caught cheating is beyond me. Maybe he's been looking for a way to tell me and get rid of me and this is just saving him the trouble. I feel that hole in my stomach getting bigger. As if I could get any more miserable at this point.

I can't stop my voice from breaking as I ask him the question that's burning at me, "How could you do that to me, Thomas? After everything we've shared? I allowed myself to fall in love with you."

He goes completely still then, and I do too when I realize with horror what I just admitted. I look down, humiliated. The man has another woman, and I just admitted to falling in love with him. You might as well just shoot me now because I'm going to crawl into a hole and die.

"You love me, Ella?" his voice comes out in a husky whisker, but I press my lips together, refusing to answer him. Of all the things I said, why is that what he's honing in on?

"Does she love you too?" my voice comes out tiny and pitiful, and I hate myself for asking the question, but I have to know.

"I reckon she does," he says softly, and a fresh wave of tears pricks my eyes as I curl in on myself like he physically struck me. How can he state it so matter-of-factly like that? Do my feelings not matter to him at all?

"She's my sister."

I blink as I register what he said. He cups my chin gently and tilts my face up to look at him. "Gwen. She's my sister, lass."

I can't breathe for a second. His sister. He's not involved with someone else? He's not cheating on me?

"But why didn't you just tell me if you were meeting your sister?" I ask him. "You said you had a meeting, and I assumed it was a business meeting until I saw you in the restaurant with her. I saw her leaning in to kiss you." I'm shaking my head as the images of the two of them together replay through my mind.

"You saw her leaning in? Did you not see her kiss me?"

I shake my head. "No, I..." I fumble over my words,

my cheeks flaming, "I couldn't stay and watch," I finally whisper.

A spark of sympathy and tenderness lights his blue eyes as he tells me, "If you'd have watched long enough, you'd have seen that she just kissed me on the cheek, lass. And as far as our meeting went, it was partially a business meeting. My sister runs an international jewelry company." He runs his thumb over my lips as he draws my eyes up to meet his again. "I was ordering something special for *you*, honey. That's why I didn't tell you about it. It was supposed to be a surprise. But I'm sorry that my omission caused you any pain. I swear to God, Ella, the last thing I ever want to do is hurt you. I'd cut off my own arm before I'd ever intentionally hurt you."

I search his eyes, seeing nothing but sincerity in them. And when I think back on him and the woman he'd been with, I feel foolish for not considering that she was a relation before. They both have the same auburn hair.

I bite my lip as I peek up at him, feeling small and petty. "I'm so sorry for doubting you, Thomas."

"It's okay, lass." He strokes my cheek, forgiving me easily. "That piece of shit ex of yours really did a number on you," his jaw hardens again, and his nostrils flare as he thinks about Tim. "I should have fucking broken every bone in his body." He takes in a deep breath like he's fighting for control.

His eyes soften as he looks down at me again, "But know this, honey," he stares into my eyes firmly, "I will never, never want another woman. You're it for me. You're all want for the rest of my life. God, how could you ever think I'd want anyone else? I'm fucking obsessed with you, lass. Shit, I stalked you until you finally agreed to kiss me."

His words are like balm to my injured heart, stitching the pieces back together. I place my hand over his where it still rests on my cheek as I shake my head. "No, it's not okay. I shouldn't hold you responsible for his actions. It's not fair for me to jump to conclusions or expect you to be like he was, especially when you've given me no reason not to trust you and have been nothing short of amazing to me."

Thomas nods, wordlessly accepting my apology again. His lips tilt up into a smug grin as his arms go around my back, pulling me flush against him. "So, you love me, aye?"

I bury my face in his chest, my face flaming.

He chuckles before he tilts my face up to him again. His eyes are twin flames as he sobers and tells me, "I love you too, lass. More than you'll ever know."

It's like my heart has suddenly sprouted wings and is fluttering around in my chest.

I bite my lip and peek up at him with a smile of my own. "So, you ordered me something from a jewelry store?"

He chuckles. "You'll have to wait to find out what it is, love."

I purse my lips out into a pout, but Thomas covers them with his own, kissing me deeply.

I instantly melt against him, and that insane chemistry snaps and crackles between us.

I feel his hardness pressing against my stomach, and I'm instantly aching for him.

"God, Ella, don't ever do that to me again, honey. I was out of my mind with worry for you, and then I show up here and find another man's hands on you." I feel his hands vibrating against my skin with suppressed rage.

Suddenly feeling the need to reassure him now, I press my lips against him, slipping my tongue into his mouth and kissing him with all the love I feel for him.

"Jesus," he curses against my lips as he lifts me and carries me inside my apartment, kicking the door shut behind us.

"Need you now," he groans as he quickly sheds us both of our clothing until we're standing before each other naked.

My eyes drink in the sight of his chiseled chest,

taking in the Celtic tattoos that span across his front and down one arm.

He doesn't give me much time to admire him, though, before he sits down on the couch and pulls me onto his lap to straddle him.

If I thought that me being on top would put me in control, I was sadly mistaken because Thomas immediately takes charge, lining himself up against me before thrusting deep in one smooth glide.

I shudder and moan, throwing my head back at the way he fills me so perfectly, so deliciously.

He kisses and sucks on my neck as he begins to pump up into me savagely, pulling me down on top of him to meet his upward thrusts so that he goes so deep I can feel him hitting my cervix.

"Thomas!" I cry out his name as I feel my release quickly approaching.

"Yes, that's it," he grinds out between clenched teeth as he continues to hammer up into me. Sweat breaks out on his brow, and his eyes are feral as he snarls, "Kiss me, lass."

I smash my lips to his and kiss him just as those waves of pleasure crash over me.

My body goes lax against him, but his tongue continues to seek out mine until I feel his entire body stiffen. "Fuck, Ella!" he hisses against my lips before he throws his own head back, letting out a deep, guttural groan.

I feel his heat flooding me in thick, hot spurts that send more ripples of pleasure shooting through me.

He holds himself deep inside me as we cling to one another, shuddering in the aftermath of our chaotic union.

If his goal was to distract me from badgering him with questions about what he bought me, then it worked because in this moment, I'm completely sated and thinking of nothing but my Irishman and how much I love him.

I vow to myself then and there that I'll never doubt him again. He showed me what true love really is, and he deserves my love, trust, and devotion.

Always.

No doubts.

epilogue

. . .

Two Years Later

Thomas

IT DIDN'T TAKE LONG for Ella to figure out what I ordered for her. As I predicted, my damn sister couldn't keep her mouth shut and let it slip that I'd ordered Ella a ring.

Ella had turned wide eyes to me, and while I'd been planning to propose to her more romantically, I went down on one knee right then and there and asked her to be my wife—before I ever even had the ring in my possession.

Apparently, that didn't matter to Ella, though, because she'd tearfully said yes and flung herself into my arms.

As soon as the ring arrived, I slipped it on her finger and made her mine in every way. It didn't take long for me to put some babies inside her either—not with the way I nut inside her four or five times a day, sometimes more. If I have my way, I'll be putting more inside her soon. There's nothing I love more than seeing Ella all swollen with my seed. A little part of her and me inside her. Visible proof of our love for one another. Another way to tie her to me forever.

Yeah, I'm a Neanderthal when it comes to her. Obsessive, possessive, insane. Ask me if I give a fuck because I don't. Nothing is too over the top when it comes to my woman.

Of course, I think I drove her even more crazy than usual with my insane protectiveness when she was pregnant, but I can't help it. Knowing that a woman is carrying his child will do that to a man.

And I was even more paranoid because Ella hadn't just been carrying my child. She'd been carrying my *children*.

I press a kiss to each of my sleeping girls' head, my heart swelling with love. Avery and Aubrey. Our little twins. They have my auburn hair and their mother's green eyes. They're already breathtakingly beautiful. I know I'm biased, but Ella and I have both been approached by those baby model companies offering to book our girls to model baby products. As much of a compliment as that is, we both agreed to turn them down. We don't want to have our daughters in the public eye like that. Plus, we want them to be children as long as they can. We don't want them working when they're barely toddlers.

My chest tightens as I watch them sleeping, their little arms curled around each other. They're so beautiful—like their mother. I don't even want to think about when they grow up and become teenagers. They're not dating. They're not. I won't be able to handle it. Shit, I can barely handle Ella wearing those workout bras at the studio, never mind the fact that I've made damn sure she's never had another male student other than myself. I keep close tabs on Ella's studio, and if any man lingers by that window or starts to open the door, he's given a not-so-friendly reminder of why it'd be detrimental to his health for him to take up yoga.

Ella would no doubt be pissed if she knew I was scaring away potential customers, but what she doesn't know won't hurt her. Besides, it's not that I don't trust her. It's that I don't trust myself not to murder any other man who touches her or looks at her doing those obscene, cock-teasing yoga poses.

I feel myself hardening in my pants as I remember the last time I walked into our bedroom and caught Ella in the middle of one of her yoga poses. Suffice it to say, she wasn't in that pose long before I stripped us both and was balls deep in her tight pussy.

With the girls fast asleep, I leave and go in search of my wife. I smile to myself when I hear water running in the bathroom.

I step inside and see Ella already laying in the water, her head resting on the edge of the tub, her eyes closed in relaxation. She doesn't hear me approach over the sound of the running water.

I quickly shuck off my clothes and slide in behind her, lifting her so that she's sitting on me with her back against my chest.

"Thomas," she purrs and stretches, reaching behind to grab my neck and pull me down for a kiss. I meet her lips willingly, my cock growing even harder at the sensation of her sweet tongue sliding against mine.

Fuck, I'll never get enough of this woman.

My hands slide up to cup her breasts. She moans when I begin to toy with her nipples while kissing and sucking on her neck, leaving my mark on her. Maybe it's juvenile of me to take such pleasure in leaving hickeys on her neck, but I can't help it. I get a sense of primal satisfaction out of seeing my marks on her, knowing that when other people see them, they'll know that she's taken. That she's *mine*.

"Are the girls asleep?" she asks me.

"Yes," I breathe against her skin while kissing her, "and now their mommy is all mine."

She gasps when I position myself against her entrance and then push inside her. She arches her back against me, and I move my fingers down to her pearly nub and begin rubbing it in rhythmic circles as I push gently inside her.

Fuck, I'm not even three pumps in and I already feel my balls tightening up, getting ready to come.

I grit my teeth and hold back, moving inside her torturously slowly as I continue to work her bundle of nerves, rubbing her quickly to the tempo I know she likes.

"Thomas," she pants, arching up into my hand.

Having her on the edge and desperate for me like this is always my undoing. "Oh god, honey," I moan as I press myself more firmly inside her and begin to piston in and out of her, water sloshing over the side of the tub as I do so.

I'm losing control. I can already feel my release traveling up my stalk. "Come with me, Ella," I whisper in her ear before laving that sensitive spot right behind her lobe.

I feel a shiver pass through her entire body before she falls apart on me, her muscles clenching and contracting.

I groan as my release shoots forth, spilling into her.

I pump into her a few more times, seed frothing from my tip, kissing her womb with every pump.

She goes limp in my arms, laying back against my chest, and I just hold her there, savoring the feeling of her.

There's no greater gift than having her trust and devotion.

I lay my hand over her stomach protectively. "I hope we have twin boys next time."

She stills in my arms. "How did you know?"

I chuckle into her hair. "I know your body better than you *do*, love. You were late this month." Shit, I noticed she was late before she did, though I didn't comment on it. And I know she took a pregnancy test too, but she's been waiting for what she thinks is the right time to tell me she's pregnant again. What she doesn't realize is that with her, any time is the right time. She can wake me up from a dead sleep, interrupt my meeting with my biggest client. I don't care. She and our children are the most important thing in my life.

"I don't know if I can handle another pair of twins," she groans.

"You can't," I tell her matter-of-factly.

She looks up at me in surprise before she narrows her eyes.

"But *we* can, honey." She softens at my reminder

that she'll never be alone again. We're a team, and I'll always be there for her every step of the way, no matter what.

She smiles up at me—that smile that still makes my heart skip a beat. "I love you, Thomas."

I'll never get tired of hearing her say that. "I love you too, lass."

And I do. I'll always love her. Not until death do us part—but even after that.

Ella is mine. Forever.

THE END

Connect with Emma!

Visit Emma's website to get a FREE book you can't get anywhere else: www.authoremmabray.com.